Serendipitous Tribulation

BY

Eidahs

EDITED BY JONATHON SAWYER & BINKY INK

COVER BY BINKY INK

BINKY INK

THE LITERARY ARM OF BINKY PRODUCTIONS

WWW.BINKYPRODUCTIONS.COM/SHORTSTORIES

<u>WARNINGS:</u>

Strong Language and Mild Violence.

Table of Contents

<h1 style="text-align:center">Chapter 1</h1>

Sam finished wrapping the sandwich he'd made for Jodie and handed it to her.

'A hearty sandwich for your long day of work, honey,' he said.

Leaning in, Jodie smiled, nudging his nose with hers. 'Thank you, sweetheart.' She kissed him quickly before heading for the door.

Sam caught her arm and placed a tender kiss on her lips, lingering and relishing the moment, his heart swelling and yearning all at once, knowing he would miss her all day, as he did every moment they were apart.

'Have a nice day!' Sam murmured, reluctantly pulling away. Jodie cupped his cheek with her hand, smiling, then pecked his cheek and headed to her car.

Sam watched Jodie drive off and heaved a wistful sigh. She was always working late hours, always so busy, even on the weekends.

Sam exhaled another sigh. He had to find work of his own. Being a house husband was a habit he'd taken on from his former relationship, having been with an abusive businessman — hence it had not been his choice. Now it was mere routine.

Sam's ex had ensured Sam would rarely ever go out or see other people. The man had isolated Sam. Jodie always encouraged Sam to get back out there and pursue his passions. She believed in him, despite Sam putting off facing the world headstrong. Healing from the abuse had taken time, but perhaps he was more ready than he realised.

Sam headed upstairs to the office he and Jodie shared, deciding to look online for jobs, and found the computer already logged in to Jodie's profile.

Sam let out a chuckle, 'Just like me, eh, forgetting to close your stuff before leaving the house?'

Sitting down, he moved the cursor, and the screen lit up. Sam froze. His heart skipped a beat before sinking to the lowest it could sink. Sam exhaled slowly, shakily, as he read the message that was on the screen: *I'll see you tonight, baby.*

The icon of the messenger was a handsome man's face, not much younger than Sam, late twenties maybe.

'Miguel,' whispered Sam as something intangible gripped his stomach and twisted.

Jodie's words echoed in his mind. *I'm working late again tonight, meeting some clients. Don't wait up.*

Sam felt himself trembling with rage. He slammed a fist on the desk, clenching his jaw.

'Why, Josie?' he muttered to himself, trying to figure out if he had neglected her needs, had been inattentive, what?

He scrolled up, and up, and up, now frantic for answers. This had been going on for months, these chats. There were exchanges, explicit exchanges, and talk of work and life. Jodie had not mentioned Sam to this Miguel guy.

There were photos sent and received. Some ordinary casual photos, and one of Miguel posing and flexing with nothing but boxers on. Oh, he was fit. If Sam hadn't been so enraged, he might have taken the time to admire the other man's body, perhaps even ogle him, but the fact remained, Jodie was cheating on him.

Sam did more digging. Miguel wasn't the only one. There were at least three other men, all of whom had confirmed dates and times to meet with Jodie, all on days Sam remembered Jodie working late.

'Shit!'

Tears stinging his eyes, Sam stood abruptly, the chair scratching the floor as he did so. He paced the room, trying to clear his mind, shaking his arms. He seethed. 'You were so confident you got careless, eh?'

He took a deep, calming breath, and knew what he had to do. He began to type. *Can't do tonight but I can do lunch.* He gave a time and place to meet.

He waited. The reply came in. *Can do. See you then. Wink.*

Sam then deleted those messages. He took screenshots of everything he could, sent them to himself, deleted the evidence of his snooping and logged out of Jodie's profile. And then waited.

* * *

The spring air was cool but the sun, warm. Sam saw Miguel sitting on the appointed park bench. The guy's facial hair was short and his brown hair accentuated his eyes, contrasting the light blond and bleu of Sam's hair and eyes.

Sam walked over and sat down. Right away he spoke, quickly and low. 'Right, I'm going to talk and you're going to listen very carefully.'

Scowling, Miguel looked over at Sam. 'And you are?' The Hispanic man's accent was mild.

'Jodie's husband.'

Miguel swallowed loudly, placing his hands on the bench to get up. Sam stopped him with a firm grip.

'She's playing you, Miguel. Like she played me. And we're not the only ones.'

Miguel settled back down and nodded. Sam had his attention.

'She forgot to log out of her profile this morning – I wouldn't have known otherwise. I saw your exchange with her. She has others, men she's been seeing.' Sam hissed, muttering under his breath. 'Working late, my ass. Maybe I've been a bad husband. Two failures in a row, that's on me.'

Sam pulled his phone out and showed Miguel the screenshots – Miguel remained silent the whole time, face falling and looking guilty.

'You are not to contact Jodie ever again, you got that?'

'Yes, sir,' replied Miguel.

'As for me,' Sam said, mostly to himself, 'Jodie is *my* wife. I'll deal with her tonight.'

He stood, and left the other man looking distraught.

Chapter 2

Sam shut the door – more calmly than he thought he would – and leaned the palm of his hands on the wall.

'Damnit!' he shouted. How could this have happened? How could he have been so naive? 'Twice, *twice!!*' someone had used him, taken advantage of him.

He must've been so vulnerable after his ex that he was the perfect target for Jodie. So why had their relationship lasted, what would she get from it? Why had she married him? Sam just wanted answers.

A rapid knock came at the door. Sam opened, expecting one of the neighbours. 'What?' he demanded.

There stood Miguel. Before Sam could react, Miguel placed his hand on the door. 'Please, you never let me explain myself. I just want to talk.'

'You followed me?'

'*Sí.*'

Well, at least he was straight-forward and skipped the bullshit. Sam considered the other man, whose eyes were a little red – that tugged at Sam's heart. He sighed, 'Fine.'

He moved and let the other man in. Miguel took a cautious look around, standing in the doorway, then met Sam's gaze.

'We've never hooked up, okay, first off, so I never slept with your wife. We never even met in person. Tonight was going to be our first time.'

Sam nodded carefully. 'How did it start? I mean, I scrolled fast and took those screenshots fast.'

Miguel glanced down at his shoes. 'My closest childhood friend died of cancer several months ago,' started Miguel.

'Shit, Miguel, I'm so sorry.' The pang of sympathy was undeniable.

Miguel waved a hand dismissively, looking up again. He smiled fondly. 'She was a real fighter. We knew it was coming. She was dear to me.' He put a hand to his heart. 'Not in love, but love, like family.'

'I understand.'

'I wanted to forget her loss. I got drunk and found myself in one of those modern, old-school chat rooms. That's where I chatted with Jodie for the first time.'

'You were vulnerable,' noted Sam. Just like Sam had been.

'Jodie picked me up and helped me grieve. We became close.'

Sam realised Miguel must've leaned on Jodie during his most difficult moments, and now Sam had callously shown him this woman to be playing him. Sam felt like a jerk for it.

'We started flirting.' Miguel's eyes widened. 'I swear, I had no idea she was married.' He glanced behind him, then back at Sam as though suddenly aware of their close quarters and Sam's stronger build.

'Don't worry, I won't deck you.'

Miguel sighed in relief, but he was still tense.

Sam hesitated, raking a hand through his blond hair. 'I suppose I should tell you how I met Jodie too.'

'Well, only if you want,' offered Miguel.

'It's relevant. She . . . I was pretty messed up after my last relationship – used and abused. I was . . . vulnerable. I needed validation, or confirmation that I was sane and that my ex had been the one in the wrong.'

'I can understand that. I know a friend who was abused – it messes up your perception of self.'

'It does.' Sam could see Miguel begin to relax and he perceived the sympathy in the other man's eyes. 'Listen, you want a cold one?'

'I don't drink . . . anymore.'

'Sorry, cold glass of water, then?'

'Sí.'

'So, how long have you been sober?' asked Sam, as he offered a glass of filtered water to Miguel and invited him to sit on the couch. Oddly, he too felt relaxed, and they sat next to each other as though it was natural.

'Since that night,' answered Miguel.

'Did Jodie help you quit?'

'No. She doesn't know I was drunk that night or that I chose never to drink again after losing Elena, my friend. She knows all about the loss, though.'

Sam nodded thoughtfully. 'That's very courageous, to face your grief without any . . . drugs or stimulants.'

'I wanted a clear mind, and I feel I have let go. I will always grieve for my friend, sure, but I feel . . . Elena wanted me to be happy.' Miguel bowed his head. 'And I found that, independent of Jodie.'

Miguel looked up at Sam, taking a sip of water. A drop remained on the corner of his mouth. Sam cursed himself for the flutter he felt.

'I'm sorry.' Sam cleared his throat, moving a few inches away on the couch. 'This is strange, isn't it?'

'Sí.' Miguel's eyes never left Sam's. After a pause, he asked, 'You met Jodie in the chatroom, yes?'

'Yes, it seems to be her M.O., where she finds all her . . . targets?' Sam passed a hand through his hair, trembling again. He blurted, 'My world's falling apart. I don't know what to think! Why did this have to happen? Why so many other men? What does she get from this? Am I that bad of a husband?'

'Whoa, slow down, *compadre*.' Miguel reflexively placed a hand on Sam's, which was on his knee, before quickly removing it and apologising. 'This isn't your fault. Jodie . . . okay, I was growing attached and hoping for something, but I am not emotionally invested in her as you are. Why would you think the problem is you?'

'Because before her, my ex was also business-driven and working late and cheated on me and used me. All he wanted was someone to order about and be his perfect lover, waiting for him at home and pining over him.'

Miguel lifted his brows. 'He?'

Sam paused, contemplating the other man. 'Yes. I'm bisexual. Is that a problem?'

'No.' A smile spread across Miguel's mouth. 'I'm bi too.'

'Oh.' The two regarded each other with renewed interest. Sam realised he was smiling back.

Miguel sobered. 'I apologise for interrupting.'

'Not at all.' Sam gathered his thoughts anew and Miguel waited in silence. 'My ex turned me into . . . I don't know, I wasn't myself. And I was still reeling about the abuse I kept realising he had subjected me to months later before I met Jodie.'

Sam leaned back, sipping his water. 'I thought things went fast, but she was so keen for us to meet, and within a year, I proposed. We moved in together. And here we are, six months into our marriage, two years together, and the whole time she was playing me.'

A silence fell between the two men.

'I don't know what she wants with me,' Sam admitted. He felt like there was no one he could emotionally trust anymore, not even himself.

He looked over at Miguel who seemed pensive. As far as Sam knew, Miguel could be playing him too. Jodie could have purposely allowed Sam to find her chats, expedite a divorce between them and—

Sam was dizzy with these thoughts and found his surroundings spinning.

Next thing Sam knew, Miguel had his arm around his shoulders and a hand on Sam's glass to steady it. 'Take it easy.' Sam drew a sharp breath. 'You looked ready to pass out.'

'I had a dizzy spell.'

Miguel's brows furrowed. 'Should we call a doctor?'

Sam dismissed the idea and insisted he was fine.

'Okay.' Miguel finished his water and stood, and suddenly Sam felt a different kind of pang. 'I promise I will stay away from Jodie.' He hesitated. 'Good luck.'

'Thanks.' Sam stared at his water, unable to process his conflicting emotions.

Miguel saw himself out.

Rebounds weren't healthy but . . . wasn't Jodie one? Rebound of the rebound . . . Sam told himself to stop those thoughts with a clear, out loud, 'No.'

Chapter 3

Sam sat at the table, hands clasped together, when Jodie came in.

'I'm back.' She slipped her shoes off. 'A client of mine cancelled, so . . .' She pranced into the kitchen, looking confused when she spotted Sam.

'Cancelled?' he asked as casually as he could.

'Well, stood me up, more like.'

Sam chuckled mirthlessly. 'Then it gives us more time together, more time for you to tell me' – he shouted, – 'who the hell all those men you've been sleeping with behind my back are!'

Jodie's face fell.

'As for your "client" tonight,' Sam made air quotes, 'I spoke with Miguel.' He sneered in contempt. 'You forgot to log out this morning.'

Jodie averted her gaze, her wavy locks cascading to hide her eyes. 'Listen, Sam,' she started carefully, 'it's not—'

'Bullshit!' Sam shouted. 'I scrolled through the messages.' His voice grew dangerous. 'Yeah, I snooped.

This has been going on since before we met, hasn't it?' He reclined and crossed his arms. 'So lay it on me. I neglect you, I don't satisfy you, you never loved me. Tell me what you get from marrying me. Oh, and was Miguel in on it too? Are they *all* in on it?'

'You're being paranoid, Sam, it's nothing like that.'

Sam leaned forward, menace in his voice. 'Then what is it? What made you cheat on me?'

'I . . . I just need . . .' Jodie stammered.

'Need what, Jodie?' Sam stood and marched to her. 'Because I asked you if you were okay with monogamy and you said yes.'

'It's not polyamory I need,' insisted Jodie.

'Then why would you cheat on me? Why would you play so many men?'

'I'm not playing them!'

'You are if you're having sex with them and none of them know about each other! You're playing *me* . . . if you're going behind my back and lying to me, if—'

'They're clients!' shouted Jodie.

Sam froze and took a staggering step back, realising what this implied.

'I'm sorry I never told you before.'

'Jodie . . .' Sam passed a hand over his face. This changed everything. He tried to maintain a semblance of calm. 'It's not that I can't accept what you do for a living, but I need monogamy and you lied to me.' Sam's voice cracked as tears blurred his vision.

'I know. I'm so sorry.' Jodie's voice came out as a whisper.

'I'm so confused.' Sam was prepared for abuse, for manipulation, for someone trying to fraud him – not this. 'I want to accept you, who you are. If I ever made you feel ashamed that you could never tell me that you're a sex worker—'

'You've never made me feel ashamed about it, you've never shamed sex workers. I just knew you'd need me to stop. I am a sex worker, Sam, who hangs out in chat rooms to meet my clients. I'm not supposed to chat with other men.'

'Then why did you chat with me?' Sam demanded through gritted teeth, his voice low.

'Because I'd seen you hanging out in there and you needed someone to lift you up, to validate you. I thought I'd do a freebie, like I do sometimes, but . . .' Jodie bit her lip. 'I fell in love with you.'

Sam shook his head, pressing his lips together. 'Don't, don't you dare . . . Just tell me you never loved me, tell me you were using me . . . Tell me . . .' Tears poured down his face. The truth hurt so much more than Sam thought it would. The deliberate deception cut right through his heart.

'Sam . . .' Jodie wiped fresh tears from her cheek. 'Had you known, would you have stayed with me?'

'Maybe we could have made it work.' Sam turned his face away.

'Would you have compromised who you are?' Jodie shook her head. 'I knew it would break you to know, and it would break me to tell you.'

'And this is not breaking us now?' sobbed Sam.

Jodie put a hand to her mouth. The two of them stared at each other, hearts breaking.

'After what Eric did to you . . .'

'Because this doesn't make it so much worse,' Sam disdained in sarcasm. 'The truth, Jodie! We promised, in our vows.'

Sam heaved a few sighs and paced the kitchen. He grabbed onto the back of a chair, squeezing.

'I . . . was selfish . . . to lie, and keep you for myself, and continue behind your back.' Jodie paused. 'Would you be willing to try to make it work?'

Sam considered – he honestly did not know. 'Perhaps had you been honest with me from the start. Because I do respect the kind of work that you do. It's your choice. God, Jodie, Eric tried to control me sexually. I would never—'

'I know. That's what makes you so sweet. I know you respect my line of work, but what you respect and what you need in order to respect *yourself* can be and *are* two different things. And I realise now that I lied to myself thinking I was respecting you because I didn't want to force anything on you. I did not respect your needs, I'm sorry.'

'Jodie, I would never have forced you to quit...I would have expressed my preference. I might have tried to see if we could make it work, but from a place of knowing and honesty from both of us.' Sam let out a shaking breath. 'Eric cheated on me and manipulated me, wanted to control me. I would never do that to anyone . . . I thought . . . I thought I didn't satisfy you, that . . .' His vision blurred with fresh tears.

'Sam, you're the perfect lover. You fulfil all my needs. But I do what I do, and . . . I'm sorry I could never be honest about it.' The two fell quiet. 'Sam, I would never force you either.'

'By lying and continuing without my knowledge, you did force me.' Sam walked over to the living room and sat where he had sat hours earlier with Miguel. 'So how does it work, exactly, the chat room client thing?' Sam wanted to understand, whether he could accept it or not.

Jodie sat across from him in the armchair. 'We're matched up and meet in chat rooms. We play roles with each other as part of the foreplay. I can have many clients at once since a lot of it is chatting for weeks at a time and part of it is cyber sex. Then we meet a few times and I . . . do my services for them.'

Sam shook his head, shutting his eyes as more tears spilled. 'And Miguel?'

'Another freebie. He was so kind and seemed to need a good . . . sorry. But he doesn't know what I do. He's not a client.'

Sam sat in silence for a while as he calmed momentarily. He spoke softly. 'I think . . . it could have worked, had I known . . . but I can't be with someone who lies.'

Jodie did not reply, but the two remained facing each other, staring at the floor, only a few feet away from each other yet miles apart in their hearts, sobbing as their marriage ended with Sam's words.

CHAPTER 4

A week passed. Jodie wanted to leave everything to Sam, though if he was honest, he wasn't certain he could continue living in that house.

He placed another box on the pile. Jodie had basically moved out, these were just additional things of hers. They had mostly avoided each other. Sam felt like he was in a daze.

A knock came at the door. Sam was surprised to see Miguel.

'*Ola.*' Miguel hesitated. 'I wanted to see if you were all right after we talked last week.' Sam just stared back at the man, unable to process the familiar concern he was conveying. 'I was thinking about you so I thought I'd swing by and ask if you'd spoken with your wife.'

'You were thinking about me?' Sam was surprised it was the first thing that registered. Then he added, 'Yes, we spoke. It wasn't what I thought, but . . .' He sighed.

'I stayed away from her.'

'I know. Thank you for respecting that.' Sam moved and waved Miguel inside. 'Water?' He offered him a wan smile.

They settled into the living room and Sam explained the situation.

Miguel passed a hand over his mouth and well-kept goatee. 'That is complicated. Especially if it conflicts with your needs.'

'Yeah, I know. We've separated – we're going to get divorced. It's not that I can't be with her because of what she does or that I can't consider sharing her,' began Sam.

'Then you're a better man than me. I do not want to share the person I'm with.'

That got a chuckle out of Sam, before he sobered again. 'Yeah well, I can't be with anyone who lies to me, not after Eric – my ex. I need full transparency.'

'Then I have a confession,' said Miguel, placing his glass down and stretching out his arms, fingers spread out, 'for the sake of full transparency.'

Sam's heart sank, and then a pang hit him when he realised it had sunk.

'I may be a teensy relieved you are separating from your wife.'

Sam gaped at Miguel.

'Because . . . well, now it means you're available.'

Sam felt his face become hot and his heart pounded in his chest. He was also relieved, and then scared.

'Of course, I want to respect that you might need your space,' Miguel added quickly.

Sam let out a laugh, a genuine laugh, blushing and looking down. He had not laughed all week. 'Well, for the sake of full transparency . . .'

Biting his lip, Sam pulled out his phone and showed Miguel the image Miguel had sent to Jodie – flexing in his boxers – that Sam had saved on his phone. If Miguel was making an obvious pass at him, Sam felt he deserved to know the interest was reciprocated.

'Wow, Sam,' Miguel looked bashful.

'I mean, you're very easy on the eyes.'

The two laughed as Sam put his phone away. Then he pulled it out again. He smiled at Miguel. 'Would you like to have my number?'

* * *

Several more weeks passed. Jodie had long since moved everything out, and Sam had stopped wearing his ring. It would be another year before the divorce could go through, though – they had to be separated for a full year. They had spoken only when meeting with their lawyers and when Jodie had come to get her things. Sam had also moved out to a smaller place – he couldn't bear to continue to live in the home he had shared with Jodie.

He wondered at the oddity of how things transpired, and hoped that he was finally feeling at peace with the separation.

Sam found himself hanging out with Miguel more and more, though aside from a few flirtations here and there, nothing more had happened between them. Miguel was respecting Sam's space, which Sam appreciated.

They texted often and spoke on the phone almost just as often.

Miguel took Sam to the cemetery to visit his friend's grave. Sam felt this was a step towards growing closer.

'Thank you for sharing this . . . sacred place with me,' said Sam. He knew Miguel visited her grave every week.

They strolled the quiet path back towards the main road. It was peaceful in the cemetery.

'Elena would have liked you,' answered Miguel.

Sam smiled. 'You think?'

Miguel stopped and turned to Sam. 'She would have loved how sensitive you are.' Miguel's sincere stare seemed to bore into Sam's eyes.

Sam found himself leaning forward and pecked a kiss on Miguel's cheek. He lingered, an inch away from the other man's lips. Miguel leaned forward and Sam quickly pulled away, turning his head to the side.

'I'm sorry.'

'It's fine.'

The two resumed walking, though the silence was now awkward.

'Miguel, look, I got scared. I realise it's still too soon for me.'

'I understand.'

Sam paused. 'Thank you.' Miguel smiled in sympathy.

The tension quickly eased and the two enjoyed the rest of the afternoon together.

* * *

Sam paced his corridor, wringing his hands as the knot in his stomach twisted further. He had invited Miguel over to hang out, but Sam wanted to take things further. He wanted Miguel. It scared him how much he wanted him, how much he already felt for him.

When Miguel arrived, Sam tried not to look like he had been waiting for him – anxiously waiting. They sat together, beside each other like they always did. Sam's hands were clammy, his heart kept clenching. He was sweating buckets, despite the A.C. being at its maximum. He wasn't ready, he realised.

'Is everything okay, Sam? You look like you're dizzy again.'

'Yeah, no, I'm feeling a bit queasy. I think we should call it a night.'

Miguel showed understanding and gathered his things. 'How about tomorrow, then?'

'I don't know, I have a lot on my mind these days.' A lot of it having to do with wanting to trust again but being unable to.

'Okay, well my next free day falls in a few. Next week work for you?'

Sam found himself turning that down too, his replies becoming more evasive.

'Okay . . .' Miguel's face and tone told Sam he had hurt him. 'Do you prefer we take a pause? Do . . . *Do you* want to see me again?'

Sam merely stared. He wanted to kiss Miguel so badly, but he was too scared to face what he felt.

Miguel let out a shaking breath. 'You said you needed us to be honest, so be honest. Just don't play me.'

Miguel walked past Sam.

'Miguel, wait!' Sam stopped him by the arm. Miguel turned. 'I . . .' He couldn't even say it.

'Good night, Sam.'

Sam watched Miguel leave, unable to protest, unable to voice his fears or conflicting emotions. He leaned against the wall, tilting his head back as tears stung his eyes.

Chapter 5

Miguel wasn't returning Sam's calls, he wasn't responding to his text messages either, he wasn't answering his door, and at this point, Sam was out of ideas. He'd apologised, tried to explain himself, blundering through but still expressing the truth. And going to the restaurant where Miguel worked wasn't ideal – Sam didn't want to come off as a stalker.

Sam went for a walk to clear his mind. The sound of screaming stopped his heart. He knew that shout of distress right away.

'Jodie,' he whispered.

Sam bounded forward, running into an alley where Jodie was fighting off a man who was pulling her hair with one hand, and with the other, pinning her arms behind her back. Sam was larger than the man but even if he hadn't been, he wouldn't have thought twice.

He yanked the man off Jodie and punched him in the gut. Grabbing him by the collar, he slammed him against the fence, seething in his face.

'Weren't you taught to respect—'

The man interrupted him by spitting in his face. 'She's just a prostitute!'

'She's a sex worker,' shouted Sam. 'She provides a service.'

The man chuckled mirthlessly. 'If you say so, lover boy.' He sneered, 'You her boyfriend or something?'

'I'm her husband!' Sam pulled the man out of the alley and shoved him away. The man spat on the ground but left the scene.

Wiping the spit off his face, Sam turned to Jodie who was quivering. 'Are you okay?' She nodded as Sam began to fuss over her. 'Does this happen often?'

Jodie shook her head. 'On occasion. He wasn't even a client. He's been a pain to some of the others, the men too.'

Sam took a step back, placing a hand on Jodie's head where the man had been pulling. 'Are you hurt?'

'I'm fine, thanks to you.' Sam studied Jodie. She smiled, 'You called me your wife.'

'Well, it's true,' said Sam. Her gaze became hopeful. Sam shook his head. 'You're my wife and . . . I loved you. I still do. It hurts, Jodie. It hurts because I want to let go because . . . I think I've fallen in love with someone else and I'm scared.'

There, he had said it, said what he felt, but to Jodie. Tears poured from both their eyes.

After a moment, Jodie smiled through her tears. 'Who's the lucky person?'

Sam exhaled a laugh. 'Miguel.'

Jodie's eyes widened, but she was smiling warmly. Suddenly it felt so natural to confide in her, and that scared him too. He wanted to let go and at the same time, he didn't.

'Sam, you once told me what you needed from a relationship, and I could not provide that in the end. I think if you stay true to what you need, you will find your answer. Respect yourself.' Jodie hugged Sam tightly – Sam held her, wanting to keep holding while at the same time wanting to let go – and whispered. 'Goodbye, Sam.'

Again, Sam felt dizzy. He watched Jodie walk away, part of him breaking inside while not wanting to go after her.

Sam ran home, heaving as he processed everything. He called Miguel. The message he left was tearful, honest.

'I saw her tonight – Jodie – she was being roughed up on the street. I called her my wife. I want to let go but I'm just so scared. Scared to trust, scared to love, because that's where this is going, us, if there even still is an us. I—' He reached the time limit and the message ended.

Gripping his phone, Sam brought his hands to his face as he leaned against the wall. He slid down it to a crouch, weeping.

Several minutes passed before he heard hurried steps just outside his door.

'Sam?'

'Miguel!' Sam bolted to his feet and opened the door. Miguel immediately wrapped his arms around Sam, who collapsed in his embrace, afraid yet feeling safe to be this vulnerable.

'I want to let go, I really do, Miguel, but I still love her and it's just too soon,' Sam wept.

Miguel soothed him with comforting words, caressing his back and stroking his hair. 'It's okay.'

Sam pulled away. 'I'm so sorry, Miguel, because . . .' He cupped Miguel's cheek. 'I want you. But . . . I'm not ready.'

Miguel's face showed his concern, hope and sorrow, and his kind smile only jabbed Sam in the gut with more fear.

'You can take your time, I'm not going anywhere.' This was a relief to hear, sending that newer kind of pang to Sam's stomach. Miguel's brows furrowed. 'I'm sorry about the other day. I don't want to rush you. I was just . . . hurt.' Sam nodded. 'But I understand. I'll be here when you're ready.'

Sam couldn't ask Miguel to wait for him, he didn't know how long it would take, but he was unable to voice anything else. He merely let Miguel hold him in his moment of vulnerability.

* * *

The seasons changed and so had the leaves and their colours. Sam was waiting for Miguel at the front of the apartment block, watching the park across the street where many folks were walking their dogs.

Sam spotted Miguel just as a woman turned the corner and called Miguel's name. She was gorgeous and opulent. Miguel's face lit up and he embraced her in a familial way.

A knot twisted in Sam's stomach – jealousy. They chatted amicably for a few minutes, Miguel and the woman. Sam found himself seething and realised he'd balled his hands into fists.

He marched across the street, calling Miguel's name and waving, trying to look nonchalant. Both Miguel and the woman turned and waved back. Sam continued until he was nearly touching Miguel and he took his hand, interlacing their fingers. Miguel looked down at their hands.

Sam presented his other hand to the woman. 'Hi, I'm Sam.'

'Christa.' She shook his hand.

'Christa is Elena's older sister.' Sam let that sink in. Miguel added, 'Like family.' His tone was pointed, but he was smiling. Sam felt like an idiot. He gave them both a sheepish smile.

'Of course.' He hesitated. Christa bid them farewell and was on her way again.

Sam turned, feeling embarrassed, and started up the path. Then realised he was still holding Miguel's hand. He stopped. Both he and Miguel looked down at their clasped hands.

Sam let go. 'Sorry.' Then he resumed.

'It's fine.'

Though Sam could tell by the look of sheer disappointment on Miguel's face, that it wasn't fine. Sam cursed himself internally. He didn't want to commit to Miguel out of jealousy, he wanted to do it because he was ready. He wanted to be certain that he *was* ready.

CHAPTER 6

Sam stood in Miguel's kitchen, watching the Hispanic man spin around and back again as though he were dancing while he prepared supper. Miguel had insisted Sam not lift a finger – *he* was making dinner tonight.

Miguel hadn't even started cooking the ingredients and it smelt so good – it seemed to warm the apartment as much as the heating did.

Sam smiled to himself and his stomach did something. That's when he realised that he was ready and had been for weeks, only his fear had held him back – the fear of not being ready. It was so simple and yet stupid and yet made perfect sense.

Sam chuckled to himself.

'Enjoying the view?' Miguel asked, giving Sam a wink.

Miguel put a plate of sliced veggies down and poured some oil into the pan. Sam stepped up behind him, wrapping his arms around him, stopping him in the process from turning the stovetop on.

He whispered into Miguel's neck. 'Wait. There's something I want to tell you.' He gently brushed his lips on Miguel's neck before the other man spun around, looking stunned, his eyes earnest.

Sam took Miguel's hands in his and led him to the sofa where they sat down. 'Miguel . . . I'm ready now.'

Miguel drew in a breath, smiling.

'I realise I had you waiting a long time and gave you mixed signals at times. You are a patient man, and I appreciate you waiting for me to be ready.'

'Sam, I . . . I want you to know that while I waited, I saw no one else. There was no one else.'

Sam knew this and nodded. He appreciated how Miguel was confirming.

'There *couldn't be* anyone else because I . . .' Miguel paused.

Sam's heart was racing. He wanted to get the words out before Miguel did – for whatever reason compelled him to.

He blurted, 'I'm in love with you.' At the exact same time as Miguel did. They both paused, gaping, and then laughed.

'I love you, Sam.'

'I love you, Miguel.'

Sam bit his lip nervously.

'So, do I wait for you to make the first move, or—'

Sam didn't let Miguel finish his thought. He captured his lips in a searing kiss, relief filling him as he finally let himself feel everything he felt for this man. Miguel wrapped his arms around Sam, deepening the kiss.

Sam leaned into Miguel, pushing him down gently onto the sofa.

Brushing his lips to Miguel's ears, Sam whispered, 'Let's postpone dinner. I want dessert now.'

Miguel pulled him down on top of him, tightening his embrace. Both let out airy moans of anticipation as they fumbled at each other's clothes.

Sam let himself be close, be vulnerable, and he let go completely. It was amazing, elating, invigorating. It was everything he had imagined and better than he had fantasised.

Breathless, Sam hovered above Miguel's naked body, admiring him. His gaze landed on Miguel's sweat-filled face. He smiled and brushed his fingers on Miguel's cheek.

'I love you, Miguel.'

'*Te amo*, Sam.'

Sam pressed a tender kiss to Miguel's lips.

He paused, eyes widening, when his stomach growled loudly. He lifted his lips. 'Perhaps we could have supper now.'

Miguel chuckled, biting his lip enticingly. Sam let out a groan of complaint, wanting more of Miguel, but his stomach protested even more loudly than before. Chuckling, the two of them dressed and enjoyed the rest of their date, their first date as official boyfriends.

* * *

Miguel sat across from Sam as he stared down at the envelope. Miguel said nothing, but waited for Sam to be ready, like the perfect and patient man he was.

It had been a little over a year now since Sam had discovered Jodie's secret – since Miguel had entered Sam's life.

Sam opened the envelope to read the letter that officially and legally declared him and Jodie divorced. They had done things amiably, and like back when Sam had sold the house, had split things evenly, though Jodie insisted Sam keep the extra bits and bobs.

Sam put the letter down, placing his hands flat on the table. Miguel put his hands over Sam's; the gesture filled Sam with warmth.

'How do you feel?'

'Free,' Sam replied. Looking down at their hands, he turned his over to take Miguel's and squeezed. 'I waited a long time to feel this way, to have this future with you. You waited a long time for me to be ready to let you in.' He lifted his face to gaze into Miguel's eyes. 'I don't know if or when I'll be ready to marry again, but I know I want a future with you.'

'I want a future with you too, Sam. We'll go at your pace.'

'While respecting yours,' insisted Sam.

'Then perhaps I can entice you to move in with me?' Miguel had that earnest look in his eyes again.

Sam grinned, feeling madly in love with Miguel. 'I kind of like this place. Perhaps you'd like to move in here?'

'My place is bigger.'

'Differently arranged. I reckon they're the same size.'

Miguel smirked playfully. 'Want to compare?'

'Are we still talking apartments or . . .'

Miguel stood and walked over to Sam, never letting go of his hands. 'Let's just celebrate wanting to live together and looking forward to our future together, whatever that future looks like.' He had voiced Sam's very thoughts. '*Then* we can argue about who gets to move in with whom.'

Sam chuckled, standing. 'I'm telling you, your place only *looks* bigger, while it's just mmmm—'

Miguel was kissing Sam and sending tingles down his spine with the way he was caressing him. Sam quickly forgot about his rebuttal – he and Miguel were naked and making love in Sam's kitchen, celebrating the future they had together, whatever that would look like.

Espoused Promise

Two years after Sam and Miguel officialised their relationship, Miguel realises that he wants to spend the rest of his life with Sam. However, Miguel worries that Sam will not want to remarry.

Torn between committing to proposing and respecting the promises made to each other, Miguel finds himself keeping this secret from Sam, which could ultimately destroy what they currently have.

Chapter 1

Miguel hovered above Sam as they lay in bed together, his kisses lingering. Sam chuckled into the kiss, humming his contentment as his hands travelled down Miguel's back. This only made Miguel want to relish this morning even more.

'Miguel,' Sam whispered, 'we both have work.'

Miguel groaned out a complaint in Spanish. 'But I want you all to myself. Tell them it's our anniversary or something.'

'Our anniversary has passed and my boss knows it has,' Sam countered.

Miguel made pleading eyes at Sam. 'Our anniversary from the day we moved in together.'

That got Sam to grin and he nibbled Miguel's lower lip. 'You mean the day you relented that my apartment was the best suited and you moved in with me?'

Miguel rolled his eyes. '*¡Honestamente!* Call in sick. The restaurant doesn't need me today. I can take one of my vacation days and—'

'The art studio is organising a big event for one of the up-and-coming local artists whose father is a celebrity. I can't miss work this week – like, at all.' Sam's eyes were apologetic.

Miguel rolled over onto his back and stared up at the ceiling. He sighed.

Sam sat up but leaned down to kiss Miguel gently. 'I love you,' he whispered.

Miguel opened his mouth to respond but his voice caught in his throat as he realised just how much he loved Sam. He cupped Sam's face. The blond man was always so earnest, so honest. Miguel wanted to devote his life to him and declare it then and there. But Sam was a divorcee, and as far as Miguel knew, did not want to remarry.

Sam kissed Miguel's forehead before getting out of bed. Miguel admired his boyfriend's naked bum before he disappeared from view into the bathroom.

Miguel whispered a curse to himself. He bolted up, getting dressed for work as well. He was quiet during breakfast, but fidgety.

'What's with the toe-tapping?' asked Sam.

'Huh?' Miguel looked down at his twitching leg, becoming aware of how nervous he was acting, now that he realised he wanted to spend the rest of his life with Sam. No longer was it a question of wanting a future together, but of *needing* to be a husband to Sam and be *the* husband Sam deserved.

Miguel had only ever considered such a commitment to one other, a woman he had dated years before he met Sam. A woman, who after more time together, wound up not being what Miguel needed. They had parted ways amicably. She had now married, and Miguel was happy for her. They seldom spoke, and though Miguel cherished her in his heart, he only truly loved one person and had never loved this deeply before.

Miguel pushed back his brown hair, trying not to look like he was freaking out internally. He smiled at Sam. *'Te amo.'*

Sam's smile grew warm. The two finished their breakfast and were out the door at the same time, catching the bus in different directions with but another quick kiss before parting ways.

* * *

As soon as Miguel had his apron on, he texted Christa to meet him during lunch. As the hours ticked away, chopped veggie after chopped veggie, Miguel glanced at the clock continuously. He needed a friend's perspective. Christa was as close as family, she'd offer sage advice.

It had been a little over three years now since Elena had died. Miguel still cried at times for the loss of his dearest childhood friend. Sam always held him and comforted him, perfect partner that he was. And that only reinforced Miguel's need to devote his life to him – officially.

Lunch couldn't come sooner and Miguel stepped out onto the terrace to greet Christa. Miguel was gushing before the woman had even sat down.

'I want to marry Sam. But since his divorce from Jodie, I don't know if he still feels the same way about marriage as he did when we met. I mean, I suppose I am grateful that Jodie inadvertently brought us together, and Sam did say he wanted a future with me. But he didn't know if he would ever want to marry again. But *I* want to marry him. *¡Dios!* I love him so much, I want to spend the rest of my life with him, devoted to him, for him to know that I'm his and only his. But what if I ask him and he says no?'

Christa stared at Miguel, wide-eyed. 'First off, take a breath. A nice long deep breath.' She guided the motion with her hands.

Miguel obliged, inhaling deeply and exhaling slowly.

'Now, tell me, what is the worst that will happen?'

'He says no and things get weird between us.' Miguel threw his arms up, his voice raised, 'And I ruin what we have!'

'Or,' began Christa, 'things aren't weird. Either he thinks about it or he says yes.'

Miguel brought a hand to his mouth. 'You don't understand. I don't want to push him when he's not ready.'

Miguel remembered a promise they had made to each other. *We'll go at your pace,* Miguel had said. *While respecting yours,* Sam had answered.

'It is a need,' Miguel admitted. 'If Sam says no . . . I will stay with him, but I will be . . . I will feel . . .'

'You've worked through difficulties before,' Christa pointed out.

That was true. One of their greatest hurdles occurred before their relationship had officially begun. Sam had not been ready to be with Miguel and Miguel had felt played. Miguel knew then that he was in love with Sam, and he had waited until Sam was ready to be with him.

Since then, they had shared two beautiful years living together. They had already been very honest with each other before committing to each other, but opened up even more as time passed.

Sam had been in an abusive relationship before meeting his ex-wife Jodie, who had turned out to be a sex worker. As a result of the lies, Miguel and Sam promised never to hide anything from each other, even if that turned into a fight or argument, else they might wind up hurting each other. Honesty was more important to them than anything else.

Christa spoke again, breaking Miguel out of his reverie. 'What would my sister say?'

Miguel chuckled. He knew exactly what Elena would say to him right now. And he voiced it. 'Just ask Sam to marry you if you want to marry him. Just ask him.'

Miguel was decided. 'Okay. Will you help me pick out a ring for him?'

Christa beamed at Miguel, eyes sparkling with tears of joy.

'We're not getting married yet,' laughed Miguel. He stood, thanking Christa, and pecked her cheeks before returning to work.

Immediately he texted Sam. *Meeting Christa for an errand after work. Will be home late.*

'There,' Miguel said to himself. He was excited and yet so nervous. His stomach whooped and clenched all afternoon.

* * *

Christa kept pointing at all the rings she found pretty, asking, 'What about this one?' *Repeatedly*. But none of them spoke 'Sam.'

Miguel's eyes landed on an ornate ring. It was thick, and engraved on it was a phoenix, its wings spreading around the ring. Sam had lived so much and risen from the ashes of his past trauma. It was perfect. Sam was the phoenix . . . and the fire that burnt within Miguel's heart.

'This one.' Miguel told the clerk the required size.

'Hmmm, we don't have it in that size at the moment, but I can put in an order. An express order can have it here in a couple of days, depending when you need it.'

'*Sí*. Express order, please. I don't know how long I can keep this secret for.' Miguel turned to Christa. 'It's not like I can tell him I bought him an engagement ring, can I?'

'Stop stressing about it, Miguel.' Christa fixed Miguel's collar. Miguel swallowed, his stomach in knots with worry that Sam would say no. 'You won't know his answer until you ask him.'

When Miguel arrived home, Christa again fixed his collar and hugged him, repeating the same words of wisdom before Miguel hurried up the stairs to the apartment.

'Hi!' he announced awkwardly as he strode in.

Sam glanced up from the book he was reading. He smiled. 'Errands all taken care of?'

'Errands all taken care of,' replied Miguel. He winced internally. His response sounded so canned.

Sam scowled and stood, walking over to Miguel. 'Is everything all right?'

'Mm-hmm.' Miguel felt like a deer in headlights. He realised this was the first time he was hiding something from Sam, but he wanted to propose *properly*. And if he told Sam now and Sam said no – but the ring was so perfect, even if it weren't for a proposal.

As Sam's gaze searched Miguel, the Hispanic man stared at the man he loved, his heart thumping so loudly he could swear Sam heard it.

Miguel realised that by ordering the ring and paying for it in full, he had committed to proposing. *What if I lose Sam because of this?* Desperation overtook him and Miguel lunged for Sam's lips as though this were the last time he would claim them.

Sam let his book fall onto the couch and surrendered to Miguel as Miguel devoured him, undressed him, and made love to him.

CHAPTER 2

Miguel kept checking his phone for any missed calls. There had been no news from the jeweller's yet and it had been two whole days now. *Express order, mi trasero!* It was killing Miguel inside to keep this from Sam. He hoped his boyfriend wouldn't resent him for it.

Miguel kept calling Christa since the other day too. It reassured him to have someone to confide in while he waited for this perfect ring to come in.

Today, both Miguel and Sam had the day off. They were lounging on the couch as they so often liked to do.

Every time Sam suggested they go out and do something, Miguel turned him down. He wanted to be ready to go pick up the ring. Miguel was so ready to propose to the man he loved and hear his answer once and for all.

'Perhaps a little walk in the park?' suggested Sam.

'I'm not feeling too well.' Miguel's stomach was still in knots.

'You know, they say when someone feels unwell, sometimes it's because they're hiding something.'

A pang hit Miguel. He gaped at Sam whose face contorted with disappointment.

'I know you're bullshitting me, Miguel.'

Miguel opened his mouth to speak but found he was unable to utter a single word.

'I know you've been sneaking about. Miguel, you know I can't be with someone who lies.' Sam locked his eyes on Miguel, brimming with tears. 'Something's changed, hasn't it?'

'Sam,' Miguel managed, 'I swear, I'm not going behind your back, not the way you think.'

Sam breathed out a mirthless laugh. 'So you *are* going behind my back.'

'Sam,' whispered Miguel, realising his mistake and panicking internally, 'I promise you, it's not what you think.'

Sam put a hand to his mouth. 'That's what Jodie said when I caught her cheating with her clients.'

'I'm not cheating!' insisted Miguel. 'I promise you—'

'You're hiding something,' shouted Sam. He brought his knees up, looking lost and confused, and all Miguel wanted to do was comfort him. 'Something changed, and you started acting shifty.'

Miguel reached out to Sam. 'Sam, *mi amor*, please.' He caressed his hand. 'I was trying—'

'Don't touch me,' Sam bristled, standing abruptly. He glared at Miguel, his face painted with a sense of betrayal. 'We promised we wouldn't hide anything from each other. You promised you wouldn't hide anything from me, that you wouldn't lie to me!'

Miguel stood, his chest tightening. 'I'm not lying. Please, Sam, let me explain!' Miguel's tone and posture were pleading. Hands together and out towards Sam, Miguel felt like his world was crashing before him. 'This is all just a misunderstanding,' Miguel wept. 'I wanted to surprise you, that's why I have kept this from you.'

'Kept what?' demanded Sam, leaning forward.

'The item I purchased,' whispered Miguel.

'Then show me. Prove it.'

Miguel bowed his head. 'It hasn't come in yet. I ordered it—'

Sam laughed mirthlessly. 'How convenient!'

'Please!' Miguel now was as demanding. 'After all this time, do you not trust me? Have I *ever* done anything to make you doubt me?'

'You have now!' spat Sam.

That hurt like a slap in the face, and Miguel turned his head to the side, shutting his eyes.

He whispered, 'I am not your exes, Sam. You cannot assume that I would deceive you just because *they* did. It isn't fair. I have only ever been honest with you. I have never broken that trust.'

'What isn't fair, Miguel,' Sam's raised voice resonated in the apartment, 'is that you know I'm fragile, you *know* trusting is fragile for me. It took me so long to trust you, to trust *myself* with you, to trust that I was enough for you—'

Miguel whipped his head back to Sam, taking his hands. 'You *are* enough, Sam.' Sam turned away. Miguel's tone was emphatic but reassuring, the way he or Sam adopted for the other when they needed it. 'Sam. Sam, look at me.' Lips compressed, Sam looked at Miguel. 'You are enough.' Miguel reached for Sam's face. 'Sam, you are my love, my life. I love you. I would not dec—'

'No.' Sam pushed himself away from Miguel.

'Sam, listen to me. You *are* enough. This truly is a misunderstanding. Something I wanted to surprise you with—'

'Shut up!' snapped Sam, his voice cold. 'I don't want your excuses.'

Miguel drew in a sharp breath, as did Sam, who put his hand to his mouth. He whispered, tears pouring from his eyes, 'Miguel, I'm so sorry. I didn't mean for it to come out like that. Oh god, I am being abusive.'

'Sam,' Miguel reassured, 'you're angry and triggered by your past, this is a normal reaction. You are not being abusive.'

Sam shook his head. 'You're hiding things from me and now I'm being abusive. No, this can't be happening. Maybe . . . maybe it's time we took a step back from each other.'

'Sam, *mi amor*, I need you! We just need to cool off but we can talk it through, like everything else.'

'No.' Sam backed away, bringing his hands up, looking like he was more scared of himself than he was of the situation. 'I thought I was ready when we got together, I thought I had moved on. Abused, then cheated on, now—' A sob escaped his mouth.

Miguel's vision blurred and he blinked. He had to tell him. 'Sam, the item I purchased—'

But Sam bolted out of the apartment, slamming the door behind him. Miguel could hear Sam's sobs grow quieter as Sam hurried down the hall.

'What have I done? I've made a mess of everything!' Unable to stand any longer, Miguel collapsed onto the couch, heaving in sobs.

His phone rang and he hurriedly pulled it out of his pocket, hoping it was Sam. The ID confirmed it was not Sam but the jeweller. What timing!

Gathering all his strength, Miguel pulled himself up and urged his weakened legs to carry him to the jeweller's.

'I've ruined everything!' he wept into the phone to Christa.

Christa joined Miguel back at home. Sam had not yet returned. Miguel had left him a few messages. 'Sam, please come home. I'm sorry I hid this from you. I have the proof you need. Please, let me make this right. Let me fix this, let me fix *us*.'

Christa gently brushed a lock of Miguel's hair from his eyes. Miguel tried Sam again.

'He needs his space. You're acting obsessed.'

'Because I *am* obsessed,' Miguel shouted as the line rang on. 'So much I want to propose to a man who might never want to marry ever again. That is how much I love him!'

The line clicked, 'Hey, you've reached Sam. I'm either working, indisposed, or enjoying my boyfriend, so leave me a message.' That message always had Miguel giggling – usually – especially if he was the one leaving a message – he, the boyfriend Sam loved to enjoy so much.

'Sam, please come home. I promise I have a very reasonable explanation.'

Christa grabbed the phone from Miguel. 'Sam, your boyfriend has a very important question to ask you. It is imperative you answer him.' She hung up.

'Christa! No! *No me lo puedo creer!*' Miguel brought his hands to his hair, pulling nervously. 'What have you done?' Miguel buried his face in his hands, wanting to hide. 'What if this just all makes it worse?'

'Worse than Sam thinking you need to break up?' Christa arched her brows. 'You need to come clean – the truth has always played in both your favour.'

The lock tinkered with keys. Miguel stood quickly as the door flung open.

'Sam!'

Sam stood in the doorway, face streaked with dried tears.

CHAPTER 3

'I'll see myself out.'

As soon as Christa was gone and the door had shut, both Sam and Miguel stepped towards each other and began rambling at the same time.

'The item came in. I can prove to you the veracity of my words.'

'It's not true I want us to break up. Because what I want is to dedicate my life to you.'

Both stopped. Miguel's heart skipped a beat.

'Miguel, my darling, do you promise me this is truly just a misunderstanding?' Miguel nodded as fresh tears poured down his face. 'I'm sorry for my reaction earlier.' Sam's voice grew harsh. 'My tone was unacceptable.'

'You've never spoken to me like that before,' admitted Miguel. 'But I deserved it.'

'No. Never say you deserve it.'

'Okay, fine, but I was at fault for trying to surprise you and it made you doubt me because of your past trauma and I hadn't considered it like that. I hated keeping it from you, but I wanted to do this properly and well . . .' Miguel slumped his shoulders. 'I ruined everything instead.'

'You didn't ruin us.'

Miguel noted the way Sam had replied and his gaze remained hopeful.

'You don't need to fix anything. I flew off the handle. You were right, I got triggered, but you have never done anything to deserve my ire, to deserve me to doubt you. You don't deserve for me to lose it like that or to take the wrongs of my exes out on you.'

Miguel took Sam's hands in his and led him to the couch where they sat down. 'Sam, it is normal to lose control sometimes. I am not saying I deserve it but that I understand my part in bringing things to that point. You lost it, but it was one phrase—'

'Until it becomes all the time,' retorted Sam.

'You are not your exes. And I know you will never mistreat me. That's why . . .' Miguel wiped his eyes and took a deep breath. 'You are right, something changed. I realised I want to be the lover who dedicates his entire life to you and cares for you in the way that you deserve. I realised that being as we are now is not enough for me, but I want to respect where you are.'

Miguel took the plunge. 'I freaked out when I decided to do what I am about to do now, because it might ruin it all, you might not want, but . . .' Miguel let out a steadying breath. 'Sam, all this is because I want to spend the rest of my life with you.'

Miguel got off the couch and knelt on one knee before Sam, who stared somewhere between awestruck and shocked. Miguel pulled the box with the ring out from his pocket and opened it to reveal the phoenix to Sam.

'This phoenix is you, Sam, and its fire, my love.'

Sam drew in a sharp breath, eyes brimming with tears.

Miguel's heart hammered away and he couldn't bear to hear a negation. He shut his eyes and turned his face away, his fear welling in his eyes.

'Ask me the question,' Sam said softly.

Miguel stared back up at him.

'Ask me the question Christa says I must answer.'

Miguel was trembling from head to toe, he nearly faltered on his knees. He steadied himself. 'Sam,' his voice came out cracking, '*mi amor*, will you marry me?'

'Yes,' Sam answered softly. 'Yes, Miguel, I will marry you.'

Both men wept as Sam pulled Miguel up and into his arms. Miguel felt Sam's tears fresh on his neck as they sobbed into each other. Miguel was overjoyed and yet . . .

'I am so sorry I caused such sorrow and heartache.'

'I am sorry too, Miguel.' Sam tightened his hold, and Miguel felt Sam's next words reverberate in his chest. 'I love you.'

Miguel pulled away and took the ring from its box. Sam presented his hand to him and Miguel slipped the ring on his finger.

Part of Miguel was worried Sam was going along with this before he was ready, and as though Sam knew – because Sam knew Miguel so well – he quelled that worry right away.

'I'm not just saying yes for you, I am saying it for me, and for *us*. I told you when I arrived I was ready to dedicate my life to you.'

A smile tugged at Sam's lips and he chuckled. He pulled out an intricate square box of his own and opened it to reveal a ring, a golden one that had the words *My darling mi amor* engraved on it.

Miguel put a hand to his mouth, half sobbing, half laughing.

Sam chuckled tearfully. 'This is how dedicated I am to you, Miguel,' Sam declared with conviction. 'This is how ready I am to marry you, because I have been wanting to ask you for weeks. I went out today and bought the ring I'd been eyeing because I realised whatever it was you had been hiding, was not what I thought, and if we could move past this,' his voice shook with the timbre of his devotion, 'then we could move mountains.'

Miguel realised there was a mountain engraved in the ring. It was Miguel's turn to be awestruck as he stared deep into the captivating pale blue eyes of his now fiancé, the man to whom he would dedicate his entire life.

'Can I place my engagement ring on your finger?'

Miguel let out a laugh and nodded. 'Sí.'

Sam slid the ring on Miguel's finger. And the two of them lunged into an embrace again, lips pressed hard against each other.

'I love you, Miguel, my future husband.'

Miguel loved the sound of that. '*Mi amor*, Sam, *mi futuro esposo*.'

Sighing with relief, both Miguel and Sam wrapped their arms around each other and leaned back on the couch. Miguel was finally feeling like his body was calming down.

'What are we like?' sighed Sam. 'We seem to have these huge existential arguments at every milestone of our relationship.'

'Can we go through our wedding without a big existential fight?'

Sam chuckled. 'We'll get through it, I know we will, and we'll be married.' Sam looked down at Miguel and kissed his forehead. 'I want to marry you,' he repeated.

'I want to marry you,' Miguel echoed.

* * *

Eight months later.

Miguel and Sam stood facing each other as they were officiated into the new phase of their lives.

'I now pronounce you husband and *marido*.'

Tears of joy cascading down both their faces, Miguel and Sam pressed their lips together, locking in their promise of honesty for the rest of their lives, both knowing that they can overcome any hurdle together, both knowing they are trusted, loved, respected, and above all, safe.

<u>THANK YOU SO MUCH FOR READING</u>

If you enjoyed this story,
please consider taking a few moments
to write a review on Amazon or Goodreads.
It would mean so much.

Thank you.

Please enjoy this passage from

The Thief & His Hunter

Book 1

The first book in an ongoing series of
Dark Romance Thriller, Gay romance books.

Warnings:
Strong language, violence.

Conor took the photograph of the tiara from the siblings, studying it carefully. His hood covered most of his face, casting a shadow over most of his features, so he was careful when he looked up again to politely meet his clients' gazes without revealing *too* much of his face.

'Do you think you can retrieve it for us?' asked the young woman.

Conor nodded. 'This was stolen recently, yes? I think I can track it down easily.'

'That tiara was our grandmother's,' the brother offered. 'My sister has always been intent on wearing it to Prom.'

'When did it go missing?' asked Conor, placing the photo back on the table.

'Just last week. After the break-in.'

Conor thought about that. Most items he stole back for clients had been claimed long ago and sat in mansions or museums. This tiara either sat in a pawn-shop or in someone's home. Conor was no detective, but he had his ways of sniffing out anyone who was sus.

'I'll find it,' he assured.

'We filed a report with the Investigative Department of Police, but they wouldn't tell us what they found about any suspects.'

'Then I'll just have to break into the station.'

The brother gave Conor his payment – he always took half up-front. The young woman smiled at him.

'Maybe once you've found it, I can thank you properly.' She tucked a strand of hair behind her ear.

Conor chuckled, flattered. 'Sorry, but I'm gay. Not to mention far too old for you.' He reckoned he was at least a decade older.

Her brother stifled a laugh, nudging his sister.

Conor walked back to the window, glancing out. 'You never saw my face,' he declared, lifting his leg over the open window's railing.

'Hey, Vulpis?'

Conor paused and looked back at the siblings.

'Why did you choose that name for yourself?'

Conor grinned. 'Because I'm the sly fox.' He winked before leaping out of the window. He rolled to cushion his fall a storey and a half below.

He ran to the nearest apartment complex and scaled its fire escape stairs to the roof. He ran across the roof and leapt over the gap between the two blocks, the Autumn wind on his face, time almost stopping as the rush of the escape thrilled him. He landed in another roll. Then jumped down to a penthouse balcony, grabbed the railing, and swung out to the next roof, one storey lower. And off Conor bounded from roof to roof to his destination.

* * *

'What do you mean we got broken into? We're an investigative branch for the police, we've got security cameras all around the building. No one breaks into this place.' Theron slapped a hand to his forehead.

Martha stared back, looking amused. 'That's why I called you. Because the cameras caught a glimpse of our culprit.'

Sighing, Theron waved for his boss to go on and show him. She played the security footage on their high-tech screen. It showed a man leaping down the building from two stories higher. He was clad in black leather attire and wearing the signature hood of the very thief Theron had been hunting for years.

'Vulpis.' Theron paused the recording. 'That's why he got in undetected. Because he came during a time when few of us were here.' He pointed at the screen. 'No chance he turned around so we could see his face?'

'Vulpis is good. Never looks directly at the security cams.' Martha pointed at a corner of the screen. 'He used a slingshot to take out the adjacent camera.'

'A slingshot?' Theron shook his head in disbelief. 'I haven't heard of anyone using those since I was a kid.' He chuckled. 'Used to practise with my best friend all the time.'

'The one who got away?' asked Martha.

'Yeah. The one who moved away.' Theron strode out of the room. 'So what's our next step? How do we catch Vulpis? Feels like forever since I took over from Barry.' He shrugged. 'I'm never going to catch him at this rate.'

Martha followed as Theron grabbed his jacket and began towards the exit.

'There have to be witnesses to his crimes,' Theron went on. 'People who've seen his face.'

'No one talks. They all claim he helped them retrieve stolen goods.'

'Stolen goods?' Theron stopped, turning around. '*Vulpis* steals them. He breaks into museums, rich people's homes. He's breaking the law and getting on my nerves the longer I hunt him down to no avail.' Theron started off again. 'I can't wait to get my hands on him.'

* * *

Conor studied the layout of the house he was to steal from. The police report mentioned an identified suspect based on fingerprints. The burglar had taken the tiara to a pawnshop, as suspected. However, someone had already purchased the tiara and the shop owner ensured confidentiality of his clients.

The mansion had security cameras and guards patrolling the lavish gardens. Either this person was a successful businessperson or part of a mafia. Mobsters were easier to negotiate with if anything went wrong. Conor usually could offer to retrieve something for them and that sufficed. Anyone else, however, anyone who followed the law diligently, no negotiations possible.

Conor crept closer, keeping his hooded head below the bushes. He'd have to find a way around the guards. He wasn't trained to take them out. He was trained to scale, run, jump, and steal.

Finally, he saw his opening. He ran in a half-crouch across the terrain and jumped like a ballerina over the sprinklers, avoiding them. He pressed his back to the wall just as a guard rounded the corner. He turn-rolled, pressing himself to the bricks and slunk along to the large patio doors.

Lockpicking his way in, Conor tentatively slid the door open. So far so good. Aiming his slingshot, he sent a rock at the security camera in the corner of the room. It turned away from the door. Now Conor could creep along past here without being seen.

Grinning to himself, Conor left the patio door ajar before working his way to the side of the house. He jumped, latching onto a windowsill and pulled himself up. When he stood on the windowsill, he grabbed onto some of the jutting bricks and scaled his way to the roof.

He crept along the roof to an empty room's window. Grabbing the gutter, he dangled himself, slid his little stainless steel card-knife glass cutter along the side of the glass and sliced the window open with practised ease. He lowered himself just enough, angling his legs, and slunk into the dark room.

* * *

Martha marched to Theron. 'We've got a lead. Some-one's tipped us off about a man, perhaps thirties, asking about a stolen tiara from a pawnshop owner. Matches the reports. We think he might be headed for whoever purchased this tiara.'

'Then it's time to crash the party.' Theron secured his gun, feeling a thrill. This was the first time in a long time they had a viable lead on Vulpis.

'Be careful,' Martha warned. 'We don't want to harm this guy. We want to take him in and question him. People praise him. And those of us hunting him . . .'

'Yeah, yeah, they're calling me the detective who's hounding him.' Theron became defensive. 'I never even met the guy. How am I supposed to be hounding a lawbreaker? A lawbreaker!'

'Just remember we want him alive.'

'Oh, I remember. I've been after this thief for so long, I *want* him alive, if only so he can answer all my questions.'

Theron gathered a small team and they left stealthily for the mansion where Vulpis was said to be.

* * *

Conor had the tiara. He wrapped it in a small shawl and stuffed it in his satchel. He was ready to make his way to his exit, and if he couldn't, he had that Plan B he'd secured earlier. There'd been no alarms. So far everything was going smoothly.

Conor paused. The corridor was quiet, but he heard something downstairs. A fast pitter-patter of shoes.

Conor cursed under his breath. The police were here – only *they* were this stealthy.

Conor veered the corner and entered the room he'd come in from. He peered out the window and saw officers sneaking along the perimeter. He couldn't exit from there.

Conor turned back and hurried to another room. It was an office of sorts – it would have to do. He ran to the window, peering out carefully.

Good, it seemed the officers were focused on his backup exit – that left this side of the house unguarded.

Conor lifted the window open, ready to jump out, when—

'Vulpis! Hands above your head.'

Conor paused as he heard the click of a gun. He stuck his head out the window. There was no easy access to the roof from here, nor to the ground, but there was a ladder just leaning against the wall – below it, paint cans. Conor couldn't believe his luck. He chuckled.

'I said hands above your head, thief.'

Aware of the gun aimed at his back, Conor slowly brought his hands up, preparing himself. If he could just bring the ladder closer. He reached an arm out, pulling on it. It teetered towards the window but got stuck on a jutting brick, still too far to help Conor down. *These fancy people and their fancy bricks.* These had served him moments before – not now.

The rush of footsteps alerted Conor to the officer squarely behind him – it was too late. The man pulled on Conor's hood, spinning him around to point his gun in his face.

Conor stared wide-eyed at the man who apprehended him. Taller than he remembered him, dark hair covering his thick brows, a thin goatee neatly trimmed around his luscious lips, his dark blue eyes vivid in contrast to the dim light that seemed to give his pastel skin a soft glow. And he was so much more handsome, it staggered Conor's heart.

'Theron?'

* * *

Theron gaped at the blond man before him, pale blue eyes just as earnest as he remembered them. He had a subtle hint of facial hair, far less pronounced than Theron's own, but enough to mark his years, and it made him all the more gorgeous.

'Conor?' Theron worked his jaw. 'You're . . . *you're* Vulpis?' Theron took a staggering step back. 'You're the thief I'm after?'

Conor grinned. 'So you're my hunter?'

Theron raked a hand through his hair, lowering his gun hand. He couldn't believe it. 'Damn, it's been . . . fifteen years.' He pressed his lips together. 'Fifteen years since you left.'

'Since *I* left?' Conor was defensive. 'I had no choice. My parents were moving – I *had* to follow them.'

'Across the country, several states away?'

'What was I supposed to do?' shrugged Conor. 'We were fifteen. Besides, it's not like my best friend was going to stop me because he decided to hate me.'

'I was angry, okay? You were abandoning me!'

Conor palm-clapped as he emphasised. 'I didn't abandon you. I had no choice but to follow my parents when we moved away.' He deflated. 'A mistake I learnt a year later when I . . .' He sighed.

Something clanked outside.

'Look, I *thought* you were abandoning me, okay?' Theron motioned towards the outside. 'You were leaving, so I decided to break up with my best friend because that was easier than dealing with abandonment.'

Conor's eyes reflected sadness, and it tugged at Theron's heart. 'I hadn't realised you felt that way.'

'Yeah, well.' Theron shrugged. 'Not that it matters now anyway.' He snapped himself back. 'We're grown-ups, and you're an infamous thief. I have been hunting you for many years. Now I get to identify who Vulpis is and track you down wherever you go.' Theron let out a soft chuckle. 'I guess apprehending you has turned into a catch-up.'

Conor grinned cheekily. 'Only if you can keep up and catch me.'

Conor leapt out of the window.

'Conor!'

Theron closed the distance to the window, reaching his arm out to grab Conor. And missing him. When he looked out, he couldn't see Conor, nor tell where or if he had landed safely.

Theron cursed under his breath. That taunt was exactly what Conor had told him the first time they'd met, when they were five. And Theron had caught him then – he would catch him now.

Theron ran back the way he'd come and down the stairs. He rushed out of the mansion, and saw movement in his periphery. He sprinted towards Conor who leapt over a short fence. Theron easily jumped over it, quickly catching up with the thief.

Conor reached the emergency stairs for an apartment building. Theron followed him up to the roof where Conor ran and jumped over the gap to the next roof.

Theron stopped on the edge of the roof, looking down, his heart pounding.

'You can do it.'

Theron was startled, realising Conor was staring at him from across the gap, arms crossed, a grin on the side of his mouth.

Theron motioned between them. 'What is this? You some sort of parkour expert now or something?'

'Actually, yes.' Conor approached the gap. 'Give yourself a running start, then leap like a ballerina when you jump.' Theron furrowed his brows, puzzled. 'Don't worry, Theron. I'll catch you. I won't let you fall.'

Theron merely gaped at him. Despite the situation, it was like no time had passed at all, almost like they had seen each other yesterday and were picking up where they had left off.

'You want to catch me, right? You want to have that catch-up?'

Theron pointed behind him. 'At the station!' Conor merely waited. 'You haven't changed one bit. You're just as reckless.' Theron rolled his eyes, clipping his gun to his belt. 'If I fall and break a limb . . .'

Conor reached a hand out towards him. 'I'll make sure you're safe.'

Theron felt crazy for considering this. He dreaded being high up, let alone on a roof like this. 'Fine.'

He backed away, took a deep breath, and then ran, leaping over the gap between the two buildings. Time stopped as the cool air whipped past his face.

His foot landed on the edge of the next rooftop. Conor grabbed Theron's hand, pulling him to him, and wrapped an arm around his waist, pressing him close to his body.

'I've got you.'

Theron had to look away, his head already feeling hot, aware that his face was nearly touching Conor's. Yet, the way the moon shone on Conor's face, emphasising the flush on his usually ivory cheeks, had Theron wanting to stare at him all night. It seemed like time had stopped, and a rush of heat threatened to make Theron forget himself.

Conor took a step back, leading Theron to the safety of the wide rooftop.

Theron stopped. He had so many questions. 'You could have tried to keep in touch,' he blurted.

Conor raised his brows. '*You* broke up with *me!* A harsh friendship break-up. I thought you hated me! It devastated me. It wasn't up to *me* to reach out to *you* after that. I was hurt.'

'Yeah, well, I was hurt too.'

Conor spread out his arms. 'Why didn't you just tell me that instead of acting like you hated me?'

'I don't know. It was easier, I guess. I thought you *wanted* to move away. I thought you wanted to leave me behind.'

'I was heartbroken about the move,' admitted Conor. 'Didn't know you felt just as heartbroken.'

'Yeah well, that's because . . .' Theron paused. His heart was beating so fast.

Theron and Conor stared at each other.

'I cried myself to sleep,' admitted Theron. It had wrenched his heart.

'Same.'

Then they spoke at the same time.

'Because I was in love with you.'

'Because I loved you.'

Eyes wide, both men dropped their jaws.

'You're gay too?' asked Conor, his surprise turning into a soft grin.

'Bi, actually,' said Theron. His breath hitched and he exhaled shakily. He averted his gaze.

Small hints of colour appeared on the horizon as the sun began to rise. Theron saw Conor's shadow approach as the thief took a step forward. He touched Theron's chin with his fingers, tilting it up slowly. Theron's heart skipped a beat.

Conor cupped Theron's face. 'And now? How do you feel seeing me after all these years? Because I can tell you right now, it doesn't matter how long it's been. I never stopped feeling things for you. And seeing you now is making me feel a lot more than I ever have before.'

Theron was trembling. He was nervous, and he was excited. 'It doesn't matter how I feel about you, Conor. We were teenagers. Maybe it might have worked out then, had we known, had we been able to admit it to each other. But I'm a detective, you're a thief.'

'I help people,' Conor insisted gently.

'You break the law.'

'*You* haven't changed one bit. Always such a stickler for rules.' Conor's tone was tender.

Theron downcast his eyes. 'We can't be together. How would it work?'

'I wasn't asking about the logistics of it. I was asking how you feel.'

Theron met Conor's gaze. 'Seeing you again . . . It's brought it all back. I knew it was you right away, as soon as I saw your face, and my heart leapt. It soared, and sank.' He paused. Conor waited. 'I still have feelings for you too. I think I always have, like you, continued to care even while pretending I had moved on with my life.'

Conor's smile was tender and it sent warmth to Theron's heart.

'Then we can figure this out, no? Now that we know how we feel about each other and how we felt back then too.'

Theron shook his head, and Conor removed his hand from Theron's face, his brows creasing with disappointment.

'I'm sorry. But I have to take you in, Conor.'

In one swift motion, Theron unclipped his gun and brought it up, holding it with both hands. 'Hands above your head, Vulpis. I need to take you in for questioning.'

Conor chuckled, backing away from Theron. Theron set his jaw. 'Conor, don't make this more difficult than it needs to be, *please.*'

'We'll talk again soon, I hope. We have a lot to unpack and resolve, it seems.' His smile turned into a grin. 'But you're worth it. Somehow, now that I know what that break-up was about, it says a lot about us. And meeting again . . .?'

'Conor?' Theron warned.

Conor merely grinned at him and winked. Then he fell back, hands grabbing onto the edge of the roof.

'Conor!' Theron screamed. He ran to him, peering down and barely catching sight of Conor slipping into an open window below.

Theron backed away from the edge of the roof, clutching his chest as he realised he feared more for Conor's safety than he was worried about catching him.

Breathing heavily, Theron waited to steady himself before making his way down.

Also By

Also Written by Eidahs

Sanguine Sincerity
(https://binkyproductions.com/supernaturalromance)

The Thief and His Hunter Book 1
(https://binkyproductions.com/TheThiefandHisHunter)

Like Father, Not Like Sons
Legacy Takedown
Of Sullied Dreams and Beaten Hearts
Butchery At the Debauchery
(https://binkyproductions.com/shortstories)

Also Published by Binky Ink

Stardust Destinies I: Variate Facing
Stardust Destinies II: The Drought
(https://binkyproductions.com/stardustdestinies)

The Hidden Cove: Pirate's Misadventure
(https://binkyproductions.com/shortstories)

Eidahs is a pseudonym for all mature written works, from thrillers to erotic romance. Eidahs in pronunciation sounds elven in nature, which is why she chose it, to tap into her love of fantasy, a genre that couples well with super-natural and preternatural, dark fantasy, and romance.

Eidahs is also the nickname 'Shadie' backwards, repre-senting the shadow self, innermost desires, and a spectrum of emotions, most notably, passion, sorrow, rage, and delight, which Eidahs loves to incorporate in her writing. Enticing readers and evoking the characters' emotions when she writes has guided her inspiration to spell many short stories on Medium and a series of books under this pen name.

Connect with Binky Ink:

WordPress Website & Blog
https://binkyproductions.com/binkyinkwriting
Medium – Main Profile
https://medium.com/@BinkyInkWriting
X (Twitter) https://twitter.com/binkyinkwriting